Taste and See

THE GOODNESS OF THE LORD

Therese Johnson Borchard

Illustrations by Phyllis V. Saroff

Paulist Press
New York/Mahwah, N.J.

Cover illustration by Phyllis V. Saroff
Cover design by Robin Doane

Library of Congress Cataloging-in-Publication Data

Borchard, Therese Johnson.
  Taste and see the goodness of the Lord / by Therese Johnson Borchard ; illustrated by Phyllis V. Saroff.
    p. cm.
  Summary: Describes how we can experience God's goodness in the things around us.
  ISBN 0-8091-6665-8 (alk. paper)
    1. God--Goodness--Juvenile literature. [1. Senses--Religious aspects. 2. God--Goodness.] I. Saroff, Phyllis V., ill. II. Title.
  BT137 .B67 1999
  231'.4--dc21

                                                                99-052516

Published by Paulist Press
997 Macarthur Boulevard
Mahwah, New Jersey 07430

www.paulistpress.com

Printed and bound in Mexico

For Eric
—T. J. B.

In memory of Agnes C. Saroff
—P. V. S.

"O taste and see that the Lord is good..."
—Psalm 34:8

When and where do you see, taste, hear, smell, feel, and know the goodness of God?

I see the goodness of God in the pink tulips that bloom in April.

And in a beautiful sunset on a
summer's night.

And in the waves of the ocean on a clear, breezy day.

And in the color of a peacock as it spreads its feathers.

I taste the goodness of God in a cold glass of lemonade on a hot afternoon.

And in a stick of cotton candy at my
favorite amusement park.

And in chocolate chip cookies with a cold glass of milk.

And in grandma's pumpkin pie at
Thanksgiving time.

I hear the goodness of God in the chirping of birds at the dawn of day.

And in the sounds of crickets by the
pond late at night.

And in the song of carolers on
Christmas Eve.

And in the ringing of bells for church
on Sunday morning.

I smell the goodness of God in a bouquet of freshly cut roses.

And in the aroma of brownies baking in the oven.

And in the scent of fresh pine from a
Christmas tree.

And in the smell of a campfire in the woods during autumn.

I feel the goodness of God in the wet lick of my puppy on my face.

And in a bed full of pillows as I go to sleep at night.

And in the soft fur of my kitten
when she sits on my lap.

And in the tickle of snowflakes
falling on my eyelashes.

But most important, I know the goodness of God in the loving kiss of my mom every morning when I wake.

And in the strong hug of my dad
when he gets home from work.

And in laughing with my sister or
brother as we play a game.

And in the love of my family.

I see, taste, hear, smell, feel, and know the goodness of God in all these things…

because God made them all.